CALUM'S BIG BREAK

For Team Boo – D.S.

To Iris, my little star, who already loves playing football
(as long as she makes the rules!) – A.A.M.

Young Kelpies is an imprint of Floris Books
First published in 2016 by Floris Books

The publisher acknowledges subsidy from
Creative Scotland towards the publication
of this volume

MIX
Paper from
responsible sources
FSC® C007785

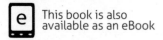

This book is also
available as an eBook

British Library CIP data available
ISBN 978-178250-265-4
Printed in Great Britain
by Bell & Bain Ltd

CALUM'S BIG BREAK

written by **Danny Scott**

illustrated by **Alice A. Morentorn**

Young Kelpies

CALUM FERGUSON

ERIKA BROWN

LEWIS BUDGE

LEO NKWANU

JANEK
POWOLSKI

FRASER
MCDONALD

LEIGHTON

RAVI
GUPTA

JORDAN
MCPRIDE

King's Park Athletic

Jordan's house

Caleytown shopping centre

Fraser's house

Park

Leo's house

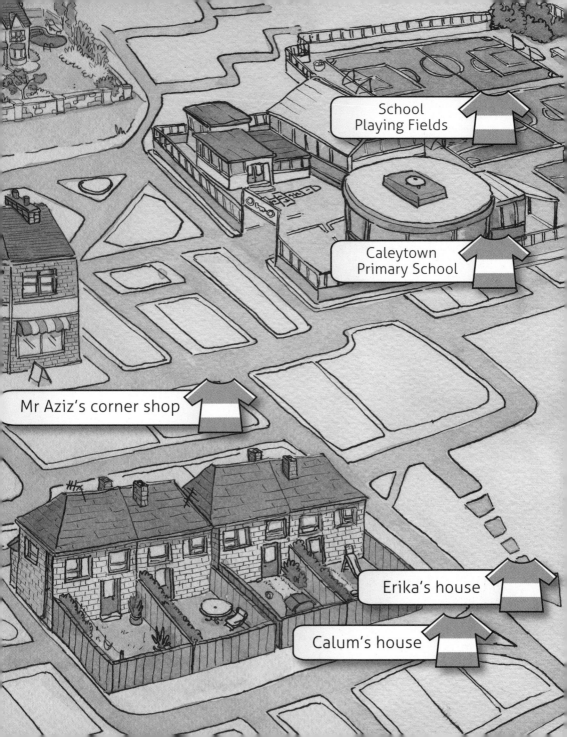

School
Playing Fields

Caleytown
Primary School

Mr Aziz's corner shop

Erika's house

Calum's house

Who's the New Kid?

"Run... RUN! They're getting away!"

Mist drifted across Caleytown Primary School. It made Janek and Jordan seem further ahead than they actually were.

Calum's legs were buckling under his best friend Leo's weight. But Leo kept shouting in his ear to keep up with them. Calum gulped air into his lungs and kept stumbling forward.

Janek and Jordan rounded the cone and headed back to the starting line for the final leg of the race. Jordan, the biggest poser in Primary 6, grinned smugly at them from his perch on Janek's back as they ran past. Janek's ice-blue eyes stared straight ahead. His face was expressionless.

"Keep going Calum," Leo shouted in Calum's ear, causing it to ring. Leo's arms were pressing against Calum's throat.

"I... can't... breathe!" Calum squeezed the words out as he went round the cone.

"Sorry Cal!" Leo moved his arms.

In third place was Caleytown's red-haired midfielder Lewis. He had a new kid from Primary 5 on his back who nobody had seen at football practice before. As they passed

Calum the new kid gave him a big smile.

Lucky Lewis, Calum thought – the new kid looked like he weighed nothing at all.

Up ahead, through the mist, Calum saw Janek reach the starting line. Jordan, in all his fancy football gear, jumped off and threw himself face-down on the ground. Janek spun behind him to lift up his feet for the final leg: a wheelbarrow race.

"Good work, gentlemen!" shouted their coach and teacher, Mr McKlop. He pulled his thick-rimmed glasses off and wiped moisture from them. "Keep going!"

But Jordan's brand new shoelace-less astros slipped out of Janek's hands.

"Watch out!" Jordan shouted. "I only got these at the weekend!"

Calum and Leo gained a few precious steps on them while Janek shook his blond head, grabbed Jordan's feet again and shunted him forward. Jordan's hands started scrambling across the damp ground.

When they reached the line, Leo jumped off Calum's back and dived downwards, sending spray everywhere. Calum lifted up his feet and off they went in pursuit of Caleytown's big defenders.

There was still a decent gap between the two pairs but Leo was on a mission. He knew how much Jordan would boast if he and Janek won.

As if answering Leo's prayers, Janek dropped his partner and stopped.

"Urgh!" Janek's face was turning grey. Jordan's was red.

"Sorry, I couldn't help it," Jordan sputtered. "They made me eat lentil soup for lunch. Come on, let's go!"

Calum could hear Leo laughing into the ground as he scampered past the stricken pair. Victory seemed theirs, until Lewis's red hair suddenly shone like a warning light to Calum's left.

Lewis lived on a farm, and he was powering the new kid forward like a plough through a field. Already at full speed, Leo and Calum had no extra gears to use. They were neck-and-neck.

Mr McKlop bent down and recorded the players crossing the line on his phone. "Whoa... It's a close one!" Their coach took a moment to watch the replay. "Right... our winners are: Lewis and Fraser – by a fingertip!"

Lewis and the new kid, Fraser, celebrated. Leo lay on his back, breathing heavily and looking up at Mr McKlop in disbelief.

Wildcats!

Mr McKlop swept his thick brown hair off his face and gathered the boys around for a team talk.

"What you lot achieved at the tournament in Edinburgh last week was nothing short of incredible. I want you to give each other a round of applause."

The team avoided each other's eyes and clapped themselves. It was embarrassing. They hoped no one else from school was watching.

"I've chatted to Headteacher Sanderson and she is as impressed as I am with your commitment to this team." A big grin spread over Mr McKlop's face. "So impressed, in fact, that she's agreed to let us enter this year's Scotland Stars National Soccer Sevens Tournament!"

YASS!

Ya beauty!

Do we play at Hampden in the final?

Jordan popped the collar up on his strip, and the questions flew thick and fast at Mr McKlop.

"Not Hampden," Mr McKlop shouted over the noise. "The finals are at Heroes Glen Indoor Arena. The Scotland team trains there on a full-size pitch when the weather's bad."

The building must be the size of an aircraft hangar, Calum thought.

"Put your collar down please, Jordan," Mr McKlop said, and took his glasses off to give them another wipe.

Jordan huffed, flipped his collar back down and folded his arms across his chest.

"There's a long way to go before Hampd— I mean, the finals, gentlemen," Mr McKlop continued.

"We're in a group of eight local teams, alongside our 'friends' from Muckleton. But it's a while until we need to worry about them."

The players all looked at each other. They'd beaten their local rivals Muckleton against all the odds in a friendly match, but now they had six more teams to play!

Mr McKlop got a printout from his bag and held it up for the team to see. Calum instantly recognised the Scotlands Stars F.C. website logo.

"If we finish first or second in the league," Mr McKlop said, pointing at the team names, "we go into a two-leg playoff to decide who goes to the finals tournament where the winner plays against the best from the rest of Scotland."

HOME NEWS LEAGUES PLAYERS CALENDAR

NATIONAL SOCCER SEVENS TOURNAMENT
CENTRAL WILDCATS LEAGUE ROUND ONE

HOME		AWAY
Hornbank Primary	vs	Caleytown Primary
Muckleton Primary	vs	Brawsome Primary
St Joseph's Primary	vs	Fieldling Primary
Battlehill Primary	vs	St Catherine's Primary

NATIONAL SOCCER SEVENS TOURNAMENT
REGIONAL LEAGUES

Highland Warriors	Fife Fighters
Aberdeen Wolverines	Central Wildcats
Border Bandits	Glasgow Steelers
Dundee Dragons	Edinburgh Knights

Mr McKlop read out the regional leagues. Caleytown were in the Central League – only it wasn't the Central 'League'. All the leagues had funny names like American sports teams, and they were the Central *Wildcats*.

"This isn't going to be easy," Calum said to Leo, who shook his afro from side to side.

Mr McKlop smiled at them. "You're right, Mr Ferguson. With that in mind, I think we'll need some extra help. Fraser, come up here."

The new kid, the P5 who had won the race with Lewis, wove his way through the squad and stood next to Mr McKlop. With his floppy hair and big blue eyes he looked a bit like a cartoon character.

"Fraser's a left-footed winger just like Leo," Mr McKlop said. "Please give him a round of applause to welcome him to the team."

Calum and Leo stood in shocked silence.

Was Mr McKlop planning to replace Leo?

3

Wings and Scouts

The game at the end was *usually* the best bit about training. But the introduction of a new kid in Leo's position had changed things for Calum and his friend.

Mr McKlop put Calum and Fraser on the same team and handed them bibs. Leo was on the other team. All the worry would have disappeared if Fraser had been a rubbish player, but, unfortunately, he was *very* good at football.

He was so nimble he could have changed

direction on bubble wrap without making it pop. His first touch was excellent and he could dribble too.

After no time at all, Fraser was tearing through the mist towards the goal-line in his fluorescent bib. He pointed to where he wanted Calum to run. Calum didn't like a P5 telling him what to do, but the football part of his brain took control of his legs.

Fraser responded with a perfect cutback, giving Calum two options:

1) He could score a goal, which would make both him *and* Fraser look good.

2) He could miss on purpose. No one remembered a great move unless it led to a goal.

Out of loyalty to Leo, Calum thumped the ball wide. But to his horror, the shot flew straight at Fraser, smacked off his back, wrong-footed the keeper, and went in.

"You can have that goal if you want it Calum!" Fraser shouted, rubbing his back with a big grin on his face. He seemed genuinely delighted to have helped.

After training, Leo and Calum walked back across the playground without saying a word to each other about Calum's goal. For once, Calum was actually happy to see Jordan catching them up – at least he would break the awkward silence.

"I don't know if I've told you, but my dad used to be star striker at King's Park Athletic," Jordan said as he barged between Calum and Leo. King's Park Athletic was the Scottish Premiership team everyone in Caleytown supported.

"You have told us, Jordan," Leo sighed. "In

fact, I think you've told me three times today already."

"Alright Leo," Jordan sneered. "Don't get your knickers in a twist just because we've got a new winger who's better than you."

"Yeah, right," Leo sighed and kicked a stone across the wet concrete.

"No, he's not," Calum stuck up for his friend.

"Anyway," Jordan continued, "my dad's still friends with one of the King's Park scouts."

Jordan saw that he now had Calum and Leo's attention. They all stopped walking.

"*And...?*" Leo turned to look at Jordan for the first time.

"*And...*" Jordan was enjoying himself.

He looked around the misty playground as if it were a stage. "He's talked him into coming to watch me play." Jordan went to pop his collar but it was already up.

Calum and Leo stood frozen to the spot. A King's Park scout at one of their matches? They would have to play really well in Caleytown's next couple of games.

"We'd better make sure we're on the team for our first two matches against Hornbank and St Joseph's," Leo said, once they'd got their bags and were heading out the school doors.

"I'm sure we will be," Calum said, relieved that Leo was talking to him again.

"That's easy for you to say. You don't have FRAY-SER to compete with," Leo complained.

"That's my name, don't wear it out!" Fraser said, appearing from nowhere at Calum's side.

"Where did you crawl out from?!" Calum said, and instantly felt bad about it.

Fraser was taken aback, but he was like one of those toys you can't knock over.

A big smile quickly spread back across his face. "Hey, are you guys heading to Mr Aziz's shop?"

"Yeah, but we don't walk with P5s," Leo said.

"Oh, ok." Even Fraser couldn't bounce back from that. He pulled at the shoulder straps on his rucksack and walked away. His big bag banged against him with every step.

Calum felt grim about how they'd treated their new teammate, but he was a threat to his best friend's place in the team. "You know what? I don't want to get a trial for King's Park unless you get one too."

Leo nodded, watching Fraser disappear in the mist. "Me too, Cal. Me too."

Strike!

That Saturday, Leo's parents had invited Calum's family to go ten-pin bowling for Leo's birthday.

For the boys, it was a welcome distraction from talking about the scout and the tournament. They'd checked the rumours page on Scotland Stars every night for any sign that Jordan might be telling the truth, but had found nothing so far.

It was Calum's first time ten-pin bowling so he wasn't expecting to win. For the adults, however, the competition was getting serious.

Leo's mum pulled her long hair back into a ponytail and bulleted her lucky ball down the lane. "STRRRRRIKE!"

Everyone but Leo's dad cheered.

"What's wrong, sweetheart?" Leo's mum asked his dad. "Can't take getting beaten by a girl?"

Leo and Calum sniggered. Not that Calum had anything to boast about; the only reason he wasn't in last place was because of Leo's little sister Anya, who was using a metal chute to bowl her balls.

"Your turn, Calum Ferguson," Mr Nkwanu boomed.

"Go on Calum," Leo said. "Pretend the pins are Jordan!"

Calum smiled and picked out a ball from the rack. He held it to his chin like his dad had shown him, steadied himself, and bowled. It looked like his ball was heading straight for the centre pin but, at the last second, it veered slightly to the side.

"Eight down!" Leo's mum shouted. "Only two more to get!"

Calum looked down the lane. One pin stood at the left side and the other was over on the right. It was almost impossible to get them both.

He bowled his second ball as hard as he could and hoped for the best. This time, it stayed straight. Too straight. It flew between the two pins, hitting neither of them.

"Not to worry, Cal," his dad said, ruffling his hair. "Eight's a great score."

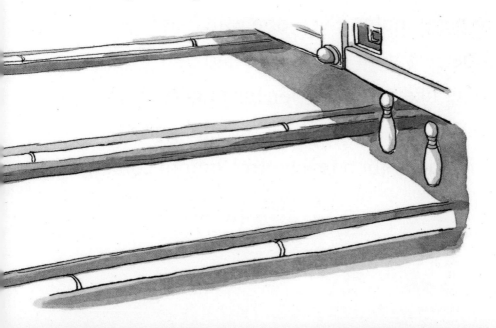

"Yeah, I'm almost level with you!" Calum grinned cheekily at his dad.

His dad laughed, "Aye, but it's my turn next!" Still, he only knocked down three pins with his first attempt. For his second turn, he chose a lighter ball. He took a longer run-up than usual, drew his arm back and bowled as hard as he could.

What Calum's dad hadn't remembered was that the lighter the ball, the smaller the finger holes. Everyone watched in pure embarrassment as Calum's dad flew through the air like a goalkeeper, his fingers stuck firmly inside the ball. He slid along the lane on his belly for a few metres before coming to a stop.

"Paul!" shouted both the mums, running to his aid. "Are you ok?"

But Leo, Mr Nkwanu and Calum were all laughing too hard to help.

They were still laughing about it when everyone sat down to ice creams after the game.

"We've got you one last present, my little lion," Leo's mum said. Her cheeks were glowing pink from her victory.

Leo looked genuinely surprised. He had already opened his main present. Not only that, his gran had bought him a King's Park Athletic strip with his surname, 'Nkwanu', on the back.

"We wanted to get you something special to congratulate you on being Caleytown's football star!" said Leo's dad.

"*One* of Caleytown's football stars," Leo said and bumped fists with Calum.

"Ok then, but how would you 'Caleytown Stars' like to watch the professionals play?"

Leo and Calum had no idea what Leo's dad was on about until he pulled three tickets from his shirt pocket and slammed them on the table.

"These, boys," he beamed, "are three main-stand tickets to King's Park Athletic versus Dundee United next weekend!"

"What?!" Leo shouted. He picked up the tickets and held them carefully as if they were golden eggs. His sister Anya looked

unimpressed at her brother getting yet another present.

Calum looked at his parents, who beamed back at him. He'd never been to a proper stadium. When he'd lived in the Highlands there hadn't been a team anywhere near his village.

With their first league game against Hornbank Primary on Wednesday, and tickets to see James Cauldfield play for King's Park Athletic on Saturday, it was shaping up to be the best week ever.

The only thing that could spoil it was the new kid, Fraser.

The Survival of the Fittest

"I don't know why King's Park bought a new striker. There's only one James Cauldfield." Calum and his next-door-neighbour Erika were talking football with Mr Aziz when Leo walked into the shop. The sound of chirping birds streamed in through the door with him. It was early Wednesday morning before school – and the day of Caleytown's match against Hornbank.

"Good morning Leo! Are you worried about this new player then?" Mr Aziz asked.

Leo glanced from Calum to Mr Aziz with suspicion. "Fraser? No... why?"

Mr Aziz looked confused. He pointed at the television behind him. "I mean the new Spanish striker at King's Park Athletic. Calum seems to think he's trying to get James Cauldfield's place but imagine what he could do for the team!"

"Oh!" Leo's frown dissolved to be replaced by a cheeky smile. "Andres Albityo? We're not worried about him, are we Cal?"

Calum shook his head.

"He's a kitten and Cauldfield's a Tiger through and through!" Leo said with a big grin on his face. Mr Aziz and Erika laughed.

"A Tiger?" Calum asked.

"How long have you been in Caleytown?" Erika nudged him. "How can you not know that King's Park players are called Tigers? I'm from America and even I know that!"

Calum glared at the television like *it* was to blame for his lack of local football knowledge.

Andres Albityo, King's Park Athletic's ambitious summer signing, has finally recovered from injury. The Spanish striker, formerly a youth player at Barcelona, is back in training and might even play this Saturday against Dundee United.

A reporter was standing outside the King's Park stadium. Mr Aziz turned up the volume.

"We'd better cheer extra loud for James Cauldfield this Saturday, Cal," Leo said. "We need to make sure Andres Albityo doesn't steal his place."

Calum tried to smile but Albityo made him think of Fraser taking Leo's place.

In the stuffy classroom later that day, Mr McKlop was teaching about some old man from history who had a big white beard. He was called Charles Darwin and was famous for his theory about how all the world's different animals came to exist. It was called 'the survival of the fittest'.

"Sounds like a good name for a game show," someone sniggered behind Calum and Leo.

Calum just wanted to snooze. He propped his head up with his hand.

"Wakey, wakey Mr Ferguson," said Mr McKlop, dropping a worksheet on Calum's desk.

But Calum couldn't concentrate on it. Instead he turned it over and started scribbling

down a team formation for the match against
Hornbank after school.

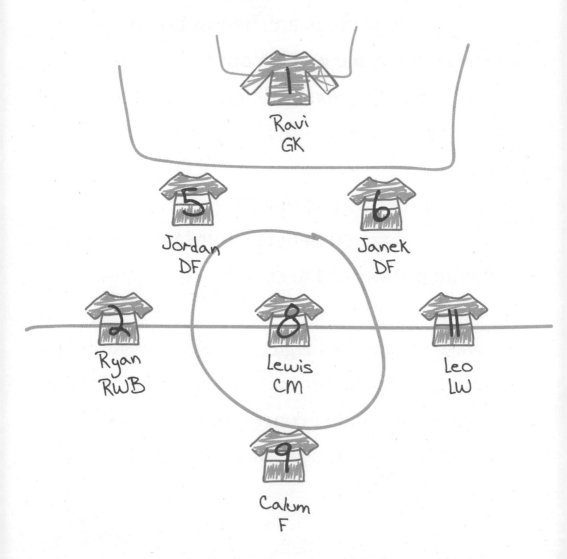

Leo saw Calum's team, flipped over his own worksheet and drew a bird's eye view of a football stadium. On it, he wrote out a formation for King's Park Athletic. Calum glanced at it. Andres Albityo wasn't on the team; he wasn't even on the substitute's bench. In fact, Leo had written his name in the car park, next to a dog poo.

A laugh escaped from Calum's nostrils. Mr McKlop came over.

"Something funny, Mr Ferguson? I can't remember putting any good jokes in there?"

Leo and Calum flipped their worksheets back over to hide their formations – but it was too late. Mr McKlop grabbed them.

"Well, well, well, this doesn't look much like the Charles Darwin I know," Mr McKlop said. "He didn't have much to say about wingers and wing-backs or jobbies in stadium car parks."

Calum and Leo stared at their desks, trying really hard not to laugh about how Mr McKlop had actually said 'jobbies' out loud. The rest of the class were in the same state.

"Leo, why don't you swap places with Chloe and sit next to Sally?" Mr McKlop said, ignoring the stifled sniggers. "And why don't you both let the coaches pick the teams, hey?"

"NOW NOW NOW!"

The school minibus passed a sign that said 'Welcome to Scunnert'. Caleytown had arrived in the hometown of Hornbank Primary.

"Remember guys, a scout might be coming today – so you'd better make me look good," Jordan said.

His friends Ravi and Lewis nodded. Janek ignored him and Calum and Leo tried not to laugh.

Only half an hour later, Caleytown were on

the pitch trying to gain a foothold in their first league match of the season.

Lewis Budge had started strongly and won yet another tackle in the middle of the pitch. Up front, Calum came alive and tried to get free for a pass. The chance came, but so did a million ear-splitting shouts in Calum's ear.

Centre... CENTRE... CENTRE!

YOUR MAN!

Right! Cover RIGHT! COVER RIGHT!

What Hornbank Primary lacked in skill they were certainly making up for in volume.

Any time the players in red-and-blue stripes stopped shouting, their coach, dressed in a tracksuit with a whistle round his neck, yelled, "You've gone quiet boys... come oooOOONNNN, communiCATE!"

And it would all start again.

Wide... Wide ... WIDE!

Your man... YOUR MAN!

SWITCH IT!

The coach's need for constant screaming seemed to put Hornbank off their *own* game. It was certainly putting Calum off his.

But Leo didn't need any extra help to put him off his game. Fraser's presence on the sideline, as well as the possibility of a scout, were already enough. He was buckling under the pressure.

When half-time came around, and the score was still 0–0, Calum tried to cheer Leo up. It didn't work. Leo only broke his mope when he spotted an old man with a moustache holding a piece of paper on the opposite sideline.

They turned to each other. "The scout?!"

Jordan must have seen him too – he was staring at the old man and whispering to Ravi.

Midway through the second half, the Caleytown players broke apart and stood in shocked silence.

"What was THAT!?" Leo's scream had echoed around the pitch and even shocked Hornbank's coach. Leo stood fuming at Lewis, whose bobbly pass he had fumbled and lost.

"Calm down, Leo!" Lewis said. He was as surprised by Leo's outburst as anyone.

Calum stood frozen to the spot. Leo had never shouted at his teammates before.

Mr McKlop had seen enough. "Leo," he called from the sideline, "come off and cool down for a bit. Fraser: you're on."

Fraser sprinted onto the pitch to take his place.

"Fraser!" Mr McKlop shouted after the P5. "Take your bib off!"

Fraser giggled, ran back over to the sideline and threw the bib on the ground. Then he trotted straight up to Calum. "Don't worry number nine! I'll set you up with a goal!"

Calum ignored him.

After the game, Jordan stood next to Calum outside the locked door to the changing rooms. He was glad Leo had left early with his dad – it meant he didn't have to explain why he let Fraser set him up for Caleytown's first goal.

Fraser's introduction to the match had inspired Caleytown to a 2–1 win, but nobody was celebrating just yet. All they could think about was the scout's verdict.

Suddenly, Jordan, who was standing near Calum, thrust his chest out like a soldier standing to attention. Calum followed his line of vision to see the old man from the pitch walking over. The scout! Up close, his face was dark and lined like bark on a tree.

Probably from standing outside in the sun watching lots of football games, Calum thought.

"Alright lads, great second half," the old man said.

"Thank you, sir!" Jordan said, still in soldier mode.

"Erm... Jordan, is it?" the old man said, reaching into his pocket.

"Yes sir?" Jordan said expectantly.

"Could you let me past son?" The old man pulled a huge bunch of keys from his pocket. "I need to unlock the door and let you boys in."

He wasn't a King's Park Athletic scout after all. He was Hornbank's janitor.

NATIONAL SOCCER SEVENS TOURNAMENT
CENTRAL WILDCATS WEEK 1 RESULTS

HOME			AWAY
Hornbank Primary	1	2	Caleytown Primary
Muckleton Primary	4	1	Brawsome Primary
St Joseph's Primary	4	2	Fieldling Primary
Battlehill Primary	1	0	St Catherine's Primary

LATEST NEWS

⚽ Super sub Fraser McDonald inspired an opening-day win for Caleytown with a great assist for striker Calum Ferguson and a goal for himself.

⚽ League favourites Muckleton scored within 30 seconds in their convincing win against a talented Brawsome team. Muckleton's Kyle Barclay scored a hat-trick, midfielder Jack Stark bagged the other.

⚽ Battlehill from Screeside reinforced their reputation for having the meanest defence in Central. Their identical twins, Niccolo and Ricardo Catenaccio, led their team to a shut-out of St Catherine's in front of a big hometown crowd.

HOME   NEWS   LEAGUES   PLAYERS   CALENDAR

COMING UP: MATCH DAY TWO

HOME		AWAY
Caleytown Primary	vs	St Joseph's Primary
Hornbank Primary	vs	Muckleton Primary
Battlehill Primary	vs	Fieldling Primary
Brawsome Primary	vs	St Catherine's Primary

Penalties

"I read on Scotland Stars that you scored another goal," Erika said. She placed the ball on the imaginary penalty spot in Calum's garden.

Like Calum, Erika was quite new in town. Her family had only moved from California that spring. Her mum had taken a job teaching at their school and was coaching the girls' P6 team. Erika was their star goalkeeper.

"Yeah, but *Fray-ser* set me up for it," Calum sighed.

"And?" Erika ran up and shot. Calum dived
the right way and parried the ball to safety.

Leighton, Calum's dog, bolted over and
started licking his face.

"Get off, Leighton!" Calum laughed. He looked up at Erika. "The 'and' is that a King's Park scout might be coming to one of our matches, and Leo might lose his place in the team to Fraser," Calum dried his face and swapped places with his neighbour.

"So?" Erika said. "Leo is tough enough to fight his own battles, Cal. Don't worry so much."

Calum only had one penalty left, Erika had none, and the scores were level. It was his golden chance to beat his neighbour in a penalty shoot-out for the very first time.

"And, hey," Erika continued, "at least you've *got* friends. Nobody wants to hang out with the coach's daughter." She pointed a thumb at her own chest.

"We're hanging out, aren't we?" Calum said, placing the ball for what could be his winning penalty. Calum felt bad for Erika but hoped she was right about Leo. His best friend had hardly spoken to him since the Hornbank game – Calum hoped they were still ok for going to watch the King's Park match.

Calum took a deep breath and fired a low shot. It flew past Erika's outstretched hand and into the bottom-right corner.

"Yeeeeeeeessssss!" Calum pulled his jumper over his head and did a lap of the garden. Leighton ran barking behind him, trying to bite his laces.

Erika sighed and pulled her goalie gloves off. "Well, I had to lose sometime, I guess." She smiled as she climbed back over the fence. "Hey, enjoy the big game!"

By the time he got to Mr Aziz's shop, Calum had stopped worrying. Instead, he was getting excited about his first trip to a big stadium.

"Match day!" Mr Aziz beamed. "Where's your friend Leo?"

"His dad is picking me up outside the shop," Calum said, rubbing his neck. It was itching

something rotten from the new scarf his mum had knitted him. It was gold and black – King's Park Athletic's colours. He felt like a dork wearing it but she'd insisted on it, just in case he got 'shivery'.

"Have you ever been to The Park, Mr Aziz?" Calum asked. 'The Park' was the nickname for King's Park Athletic's home ground. It held about 20,000 people.

The shopkeeper smiled. "Many times. My son and I used to have season tickets... have I never told you that?"

Calum shook his head. "What was it like?"

"We loved it." Mr Aziz smiled at the memory. "When my son was your age he wanted to be the next Andrew McPride!"

The gears in Calum's brain clicked into place. "*McPride?* No way! Jordan's dad?"

Just then, the bell chimed above Mr Aziz's door. Calum turned round to see the silhouette of a boy in the doorway.

"Hi Calum! Nice scarf! Are you going to the Dundee United match? King's Park versus Dundee United? At The Park?"

Calum sighed. It was *Fray-ser*.

"Hello Fraser. How's Scotland's future winger?" Mr Aziz smiled in recognition. "I heard you scored on your debut?"

Calum felt a pang of jealousy spread through his chest. Mr Aziz was *his* friend.

"I did, Mr Aziz, I did." Fraser grabbed a can of juice out of the fridge. "Did Calum tell you that? It was all down to him really." Fraser's eyes shone at Calum.

Calum rolled his eyes in response. Mr Aziz saw him do it and gave Calum a look like a disappointed granddad.

When he heard Leo's dad's car horn tooting outside, Calum tried to slip away, but Fraser caught up with him.

"I'll chum you out, Calum. Thanks Mr Aziz! This can's super cold!"

Mr Aziz chuckled and waved them off.

The sun was blinding as Calum emerged
from the shop with Fraser in tow. Leo got out
of the front seat of his dad's car to sit in the
back with his friend. He was wearing his new
King's Park Athletic strip over a hoodie and was
singing as he swung the car door open.

"There's only one James Cauldfield, one
James Caaaauuu...."

Leo's smile fell like a dropped birthday cake
when he saw who was with Calum.

The Tiger's Roar

Leo's dad's car was cold and quiet. The silence was only broken by the click-clack of the car's indicators and Mr Nkwanu's grunts – his back was still sore from their ten-pin bowling the weekend before.

Calum wished he had a computer that could tell him exactly what he needed to say to make up with Leo. Instead, when he couldn't stand the silence any more, he loosened his scarf and started rambling. "Fraser just came in while I was talking to Mr Aziz! He lives near me. Honest Leo, we're not friends or anything..."

"The Scotland Stars match report made it sound like you were best buds when *Fray-ser* set you up for a goal against Hornbank," Leo said to the window.

"Sorry Leo... but it was 0–0. I thought you'd want us to win."

Leo just grunted.

"Calum's right, Leo," Mr Nkwanu chimed in. "Like I told you on the car ride home from Scunnert: the team is always the most important thing."

Leo slouched in his seat. Silence returned like the tide creeping up a beach, until Mr

Nkwanu couldn't handle it any more.

"Come on boys! Cheer up. Today is your first time at a stadium!" He grinned at them in the rear-view mirror.

But it didn't work. Calum hadn't realised how hacked off Leo was about the goal he'd scored against Hornbank.

"Calum," Mr Nkwanu tried again, "do you like music?"

"Oh no." Leo squirmed in his seat.

"Erm... yeah, I guess so?" Calum answered, glancing at his friend.

"Ok, I'm going to bet you a half-time pie that you will dance to this." Mr Nkwanu pressed a button on the steering wheel and the car filled with music Calum hadn't heard before, in a language he didn't understand. "Now, this is proper music, isn't it Calum?!"

He was right. Before long, Calum found that his foot had started tapping to the music's beat. Leo overcame his embarrassment and started to jig too, under his seatbelt.

"See," Leo's dad laughed, "I told you, you just *have* to dance to this music."

Soon, the trickle of football fans on the streets became a deluge of King's Park Athletic supporters in gold and black. Their noise drifted into the car and mixed with the music.

Mr Nkwanu stopped bopping and reversed the car into a space.

Leo and Calum, however, were still dancing away in the back when they spotted a girl on the side of the road pointing and laughing at them. It was Sally from school! They ducked down below the car window but it was far too late. Their whole class would know about their dance moves come Monday.

As they neared the stadium, Calum spotted stalls that were selling match-day programmes, and Tigers scarves and strips. In the distance he could hear the crowd, their chanting and singing echoing like the roar of waves.

He felt Leo tug at his sleeve. His friend was pointing at a group of guys dressed in tiger onesies. "Next time, we're wearing those," he said.

Calum laughed. It felt good to hear Leo say 'next time'.

The stadium loomed up on them like a waking giant between two blocks of tenement flats. Police on horseback smiled at their wide-eyed faces as they trotted past. Up ahead, someone let off an air horn.

"Stay close now," Mr Nkwanu said as he pulled the tickets from his wallet and shepherded them through the turnstile.

Their silver foil badges made little rainbows when the sun hit them.

"This way, we're in section B1," Leo said. "I was looking at the stadium map last night on Mum's phone." Calum and Leo attacked the stairs.

"Slow down, boys," Mr Nkwanu panted. "You'll get yourselves lost."

The chanting was louder now. Calum could just about make it out. It sounded like the James Cauldfield song Leo had been singing outside Mr Aziz's.

There was only one flight of steps to go.

Calum tried to imagine what it would feel like to be a player running out of a tunnel and onto the pitch.

Three steps to go. Calum could see the crowd on the other side of the stadium.

Two steps to go. Calum could see the green of the pitch.

One last step. The whole stadium, and all its noise and colour, came into view.

Calum and Leo stopped in their tracks to take it all in.

"There's Only One James Cauldfield!"

"There's only one James Cauldfield,
One Ja-ames Caaaaauldfield,
There's only one Jamie Ca-auldfield."

Singing echoed around The Park and James Cauldfield responded by flying about the pitch like he was in a cup final. Calum's half-time pie felt like a restless toad in his stomach, but he was too excited to care. He nudged

Leo and pointed with greasy fingers at James Cauldfield's rival Andres Albityo emerging from the dugout to warm up on the sideline.

The crowd clapped Albityo as he ran down the sideline, but Calum and Leo kept singing James Cauldfield's name.

"I feel a bit sick," Leo said, half-standing to get a look at Albityo. He had a ring of pie grease around his lips.

"Me too," Calum said, before letting out a small burp. It almost turned into a full-on barf when the man behind them suddenly started shouting again.

"COME ON KING'S PARK! SHOW UNITED HOW TO STICK ONE IN THE ONION SACK!"

The man had spent the whole of the first half screaming out the strangest stuff. Calum even wondered if he might be Hornbank Primary's noisy coach from earlier that week. Whoever he was, with the score still 0–0, his random shouts had been the most entertaining thing about the match so far.

"COME ON TIGERS! THIS IS LIKE WATCHING A BUNCH OF KITTENS PLAY WITH A BALL OF WOOL!"

Leo turned away from Andres Albityo and slumped back down in his seat, as if the weight of his thoughts was too heavy for him to carry on standing. "Do you think Fraser's a better winger than me?" he asked.

Calum was taken aback. "No, you're miles better!"

Leo shook his head. "I don't know about that – *Fray-ser* is pretty handy."

"Yeah... but... it's like Mr McKlop said, he only brought Fraser along because we need more players," Calum said. "It's not 'cause he's better."

On the pitch, a King's Park midfielder went shoulder to shoulder with a Dundee United defender and flew over the sideline. Fans all around Calum jumped up to roar their disapproval but the loud man behind them drowned everyone out.

"REFEREE! THIS IS FOOTBALL, NOT SUMO WRESTLING!"

The angry noise rose from the crowd and floated out of the stadium like steam from a boiling pot of water.

To Calum, the tackle had seemed like a fair challenge. *Perhaps I'm not a proper King's Park fan yet,* he thought to himself.

"I think Mr McKlop will start picking

whoever's playing better," Leo continued where he'd left off. "After the Hornbank game, that's Fraser, not me. And Jordan McNumpty reckons the scout's coming next week."

Calum feared that Leo was right. What could they do though? It'd be lame to *ask* Mr McKlop to pick Leo instead of Fraser.

Down on the sideline, Andres Albityo took his tracksuit off and listened to his manager's instructions. It looked like the end of James Cauldfield's game. But with perfect timing, Cauldfield intercepted a pass and cut across the pitch towards the box. Dundee United's players backed off and backed off until Cauldfield had no choice but to pull the trigger.

The ground exploded with cheers as Cauldfield's twenty-yard shot glanced off the post and into the net. The striker ran to the corner of the park with his arms outstretched until he was mauled down by the rest of the Tigers.

**SS!"**

Calum and Leo jumped up and down, shouting and hugging. Mr Nkwanu was shaking both fists in the air and roaring at the sky. The stadium announcer's voice boomed out through the speakers:

"Scorer of King's Park Athletic's goal, after 69 minutes, Jaaaaaaaammmmmes Cauldfield!"

Another cheer went up from the fans.

Now he had roared like a Tiger, Calum felt like a proper King's Park Athletic fan after all. His throat tingled and his ears were ringing. It felt fantastic! "Imagine scoring in front of a crowd like this," he said to no one in particular.

Leo nodded.

Andres Albityo disappeared back into the dugout and the man behind them bellowed once again:

"AYE, YOUR TIME WILL COME, SON! THERE'S ONLY ONE JAMES CAULDFIELD!"

Lost and Found

After such a dream ending to the game, the stadium's toilets smelled like something out of a nightmare. Calum and Leo jostled their way over to the sinks and washed their hands in cold water with a sneeze of pink soap from the dispenser.

"Come on, let's get out of here," Leo said. Calum followed, cold water dripping from his fingers.

Leo's dad was waiting by one of the two

entrances to the toilets. In their hurry, Leo and Calum left by the wrong one and stepped into a moving forest of grown-ups making their way out of the stadium. They looked around for Mr Nkwanu but it was impossible to find anyone in such a big, fast-moving crowd.

Instead, they found themselves completely lost.

"What do we do?" Calum said as they were jostled along the stadium concourse.

"I don't know," Leo said; his eyes were wide. "In movies they always split up and look in different directions."

"I don't want to do that," Calum said. He felt prickles up his back.

"Nah, me neither. Let's stick together." Leo pulled Calum to the side of the crowd where they could catch their breath.

Calum saw the guys in tiger onesies walking towards them. One of them had spilled ketchup on his chest so it looked like he'd been hit by an arrow. They were all roaring with laughter and shoving each other about. The biggest tiger almost knocked Calum off his feet as they went past.

"Sorry, wee man!" he said, but his friends just kept on walking.

The crowd began to thin out but the boys were still totally lost – until a familiar voice shouted, "Calum... Leo!"

It wasn't the booming voice of Leo's dad, however. It was the squeaky yell of Sally from their class. She came over to them with her dad. "Finally stopped dancing?" She laughed, her blue eyes mischievous under her dark fringe.

Calum and Leo stood in wide-eyed silence.

"Wait. Are you *lost*?"

Sally and her dad walked Calum and Leo to the ticket office and said their goodbyes. They had to rush Sally back to her mum and stepdad's for dinner. Her dad reassured the boys that they would put an announcement out on the loudspeakers and Leo's dad would come and get them in no time.

"Are you boys warm enough? Let me get you a hot drink while you wait." A woman fussed over them inside the warm office.

She told them to sit by a radiator until she returned with two King's Park Athletic mugs filled with a steaming brown liquid.

"Thanks..." Calum said, eyeing his drink suspiciously. It looked like black coffee but it smelled like gravy.

"Wha—" began Leo.

"It's a beef drink! Have you never tried it?
It's the traditional thing at Scottish football
games." The woman smiled, before heading
back to her computer.

"It smells like a cow burping and farting at
the same time," Leo whispered in Calum's ear,
almost causing him to spill his drink.

Through the steam from his mug Calum saw
a man enter the office with a bunch of flowers.
A smell of shower gel and pollen cut through
the beefy stink.

"It's James Cauldfield!" Calum said out loud
before he could stop himself.

The man turned round, looked at Calum and laughed. "That's my name! Nice scarf by the way."

Questions
and Answers

The ticket-office woman looked up at James with a massive smile on her face.

"Thanks for sorting out the tickets for my uncle and auntie," the King's Park star striker said. "These are for you."

"Oh, it was nothing." The woman behind the counter blushed.

"It's actually James Cauldfield," Leo blurted out.

Again, James Cauldfield turned round. "You guys would be really useful if I ever forgot my own name." He grinned.

"Great goal today!" Calum beamed.

"What's it like to score a goal at the Park?" Leo asked excitedly.

"What's it like to play for Scotland?" they asked together.

James Cauldfield smiled and came over to chat to them. Calum pinched his own arm to make sure he wasn't still in bed, dreaming this whole day.

Cauldfield answered the boys' questions about playing for Scotland and what it was like to score a goal in front of thousands of people.

But it was obvious that there was only one question Leo really wanted to ask. Calum heard his friend take a deep breath.

"Are you worried about Andres Albityo?"

For Cauldfield, it was like an unexpected tackle. He took a moment to adjust. "You know what, Leo, at first I was really angry and let the gaffer know about it."

"What's a gaffer?" Leo asked with a frown.

"It's what footballers call their manager," James Cauldfield said. "Anyway, the gaff— the manager sat me down and told me that they weren't buying Albityo because they didn't think I was good enough..."

Calum looked outside and saw Leo's dad stomp past the ticket-office window.

"He said that adding in a bit of competition for places would make us all try harder in training. And it's worked. I've stopped taking

my place in the team for granted, and started training much harder, which paid off today – for the whole team."

Leo was listening so hard he didn't notice his dad tumble through the door. "Leo Nkwanu, where have you been?" his voice boomed out, but he stopped in his tracks when he saw who was there.

Calum couldn't resist asking one last question. "Fancy coming to our next home game, James Cauldfield?"

The footballer laughed. "Who do you play for?"

"Your old school," Leo answered proudly, "Caleytown Primary! We've got new strips and everything. *And* a King's Park scout is coming to our next match."

"If that's the case," James Cauldfield grinned, "maybe I'll see you lads there."

"Come on guys, let's give Mr Cauldfield a chance to catch his breath," said Leo's dad. "Thank you for looking after them." Mr Nkwanu shook James Cauldfield's hand and smiled at the woman behind the desk before shoving the boys out the door.

"You never met James Cauldfield!"

"You never met James Cauldfield," Jordan scoffed.

The team was getting ready for Caleytown's second match of their campaign, this time against St Joseph's. It was their first Scotland Stars league game at home.

"We did so," Leo said defiantly. Calum nodded in support.

"No one in school believes you."

"We don't care."

"If you're lying, I'll find out," Jordan said, looking around the changing room at Ravi, Janek, Lewis and the rest of the squad, to make sure he had everyone's attention. "'Cause my dad and James Cauldfield text each other all the time."

Leo stayed quiet for a moment, then burst out laughing. Calum didn't. He wondered if Jordan was telling the truth for once. Plus, over Jordan's shoulder, Calum could see Fraser, with his boots on already, sitting alone. Just looking at him made Calum feel lonely.

"Are we all ready to go?" said Janek. He was clearly keen to get out on the pitch.

"Hold on!" Jordan said.

There were a few sighs as everyone sat down. Jordan, as always, had lots of special football gear to put on. As well as his thermals, he had to adjust his special shin pads and tape up his socks to hold them in place. Then, to finish, he added a small black chip to a pouch in his thermal top.

"What's that?" Leo asked with his arms crossed.

Jordan looked pleased that Leo had asked. "It's a microchip that links up to an app on my dad's phone. It tells him how far I've run so he can show the scout my stats."

"Does it track how long it takes you to get ready?" Leo raised an eyebrow.

Calum tried to cover his laughter with a cough.
Jordan stormed out the door.

The squad jogged across the playground into a strong wind. Calum scanned the crowd for James Cauldfield. He wasn't there, but the rumours about his potential appearance had ensured that most of P6, some of P7 and lots of parents and teachers had turned up.

Leighton's excited bark immediately let Calum know where his mum was. He looked over and saw her standing next to Leo's parents, who were waving.

Jordan's dad, former King's Park hero Andrew McPride, was tapping away at his phone on the sideline too. *Maybe he's texting*

James Cauldfield, or the scout! Calum thought, but then he remembered Jordan's stupid tracking app.

"Glad you could finally join us, gentlemen," Mr McKlop said. "What took you so long?"

Everyone glanced at Jordan.

"Anyway, now that you're all here..."

Lewis's hand shot up in the air.

"Yes Mr Budge?" Mr McKlop pushed up his glasses.

"I know something about our opponents, sir," said Lewis.

"What do you know?" Mr McKlop folded his arms.

"My cousin Kieran plays for them. He says

they're amazing in attack but don't really do much defending."

The Caleytown boys all looked across the pitch at the other team huddled round in their sky-blue shirts and white shorts. It didn't take long to figure out who Lewis's cousin was. The red hair gave it away.

"Well let's bear that in mind, gentlemen."
Mr McKlop smiled. "Ok guys, grab your strips as
I call your names."

The squad held its collective breath.

"Ravi in goal. Jordan McPride and Janek
Powolski in defence."

Ravi carefully pulled the goalie top over
his precious quiff. Jordan pulled his number
five strip on gently, so as not to dislodge his
microchip. Calum didn't even see Janek put
on his strip – the big defender always seemed
ready for anything.

"Right wing back, Ryan Castor," Mr McKlop
said. "You need to make sure you don't leave
gaps at the back. Understood, Mr Castor?"

Ryan nodded, grabbed his number two jersey and dropped it over his wiry frame.

"Central midfielder, Lewis. Enjoy playing your cousin, sir." Mr McKlop smiled.

Lewis bounced over to the kitbag like a pneumatic drill and grabbed his favourite number eight strip.

"Left wing, Fraser. And up front, Calum," Mr McKlop said. "Sorry Leo, you'll get on soon enough, I promise."

Calum opened his mouth to protest but Leo cut him off by shouting, "Come on Caleytown! Let's get another three points on the board."

Mr McKlop nodded his approval.

It's Showtime!

"Are you left-footed or right-footed?" Fraser asked Calum at the centre spot.

"Figure it out," Calum said with a sneer. Scout or no scout, Calum was furious that Fraser had taken his friend's place.

PEEEeeeeEEP

Calum passed the ball back to Lewis, whose cousin, Kieran, tore after him like a hungry hunting dog. After a wild blur of red hair, feet,

elbows and grins the ball finally pinged off Lewis's boot in the direction of Fraser.

Fraser's face lit up and he flew forward like he was on one of those moving walkways at the airport. Meanwhile Lewis broke free of his cousin's grasp long enough to bark for a return pass. He and Fraser played a quick one-two.

Calum just stood next to a St Joseph's defender and watched Fraser glide down the pitch. Even Jordan flew past him into the box, screaming for a cutback, but Fraser spotted a better option. He flashed a shot across the goal, right past St Joseph's baseball-cap-wearing keeper and into the far side of the net.

There was no sign of a scout yet, but Jordan was still unimpressed. He shook his head at Fraser and jogged back. His team's 1–0 lead didn't lift Calum's spirits much either.

"Thanks for staying back to make space, Calum," said Fraser with a genuine grin.

Calum, who'd done no such thing, only grunted. But St Joseph's weren't interested in Caleytown's problems. And Lewis's cousin wasn't lying about their ability to attack. Despite having the wind in their faces, they swarmed forward, leaving Jordan, Janek and Ryan to chase their shadows.

The ball found its way to Kieran Budge, who had a clear sight of goal. Ravi's quiff seemed to swell as he bounced on his tiptoes, ready to leap in either direction. Lewis's cousin got lucky – his mis-hit sent Caleytown's stopper the wrong way to make it 1–1. He ruffled Lewis's hair on his way back to his own half.

Fraser helped Lewis get his revenge minutes later by setting him up with an easy tap-in to put Caleytown back in the lead at 2–1. Lewis gave Kieran a rough shove to celebrate, and high-fived Fraser in the box.

Still Calum didn't feel like joining in the celebrations. He even wished Mr McKlop would just take him off when, minutes later, he gave the ball away allowing St Joseph's to make it 2–2.

Special guest or not, the crowd cheered and clapped both teams off after a four-goal first half.

Caleytown's men of the match so far, Fraser and Lewis, got several slaps on the back for their performances. Fraser's face beamed

and Lewis showed everyone the cuts and bruises his cousin had inflicted upon him, proudly, as if they were medals.

Leo came running over to Calum with a water bottle.

"Thanks, but I'm not thirsty," Calum said.

"No wonder, you need to run to get thirsty," Leo said.

"Maybe if you were on the pitch instead of Fraser, I would," Calum moaned.

Leo shrugged. "Thanks Cal – but you losing your place on the team doesn't get me mine back."

Calum kicked a bottle over in frustration. Mr McKlop pretended not to notice.

"Remember what James Cauldfield said about Andres Albityo," Leo continued. "I just need to make myself un-droppable, like he has!"

Calum wanted to change the subject. "Spotted a scout?"

"Not yet," Leo said. A grin spread over his face. "He must be waiting for *me* to get on."

Half-time was almost over by the time Mr McKlop gathered the team. He had spent the break staring across the pitch at St Joseph's, his brown hair flopping this way and that in the wind. Finally, he spoke.

"Sharing the Central Wildcats league with

Muckleton means we can't afford to drop too many points – especially at home." Mr McKlop looked across the pitch at St Joseph's one last time. "That's why we're going to outscore this lot, gentlemen. Leo, take your bib off, you're on."

"Yes!" Calum punched the air.

Leo reacted like it was no big deal. He pulled his bib off to reveal the number fourteen on his back.

Fraser, on the other hand, looked at Mr McKlop like he had just cancelled his birthday. He plodded over to grab a bib from the bag.

"What are you doing Fraser? I said we're going to outscore them," Mr McKlop repeated. He turned to Ryan. "Ryan, good shift, I'll get you back on later. Fraser, try the right wing; Leo, left-wing."

Fraser's face lit back up like floodlights after a power cut.

Calum, suddenly feeling like anything was possible, sprinted on the spot and blew warm air on his cold hands.

"It's showtime, Caleytown!" Mr McKlop sent the team back onto the pitch to a big cheer.

Wings

As St Joseph's were getting ready to kick off, Calum spotted two men making their way across the playground.

"Look who it is!" Leo shouted to Calum. He'd noticed them too.

Seeing James Cauldfield again reminded Calum of the star's wise words at the stadium. Calum walked over to where Fraser was standing in position and tapped him on the shoulder. The P5 whipped round with a grimace, like he was expecting something to hurt.

"I'm not left-footed or right-footed," Calum said. "Either's good."

A smile spread across Fraser's face like sunlight across a football pitch. "Ace!"

PEEEEEP!

Lewis Budge shot forward to restart his

family feud. Kieran simply sidestepped him and Lewis flew face-first into the Astroturf.

With the wind now at his back, Lewis's cousin strode forward and tried his luck with a long-range shot.

Even Ravi's quiff was struggling to stay in one position for long in the strong gusts. The ball moved this way and that before evading his fingertips to fly into the net. St Joseph's now led 3–2.

Leo yelled for a pass straight from the restart. Calum squared it to him and he tore up the pitch as if the past two weeks hadn't happened.

Like a mountain skier, Leo slalomed between the defending St Joseph's players, who must have wondered why he had been a substitute all this time. St Joseph's keeper came out and made himself big, but Leo just rolled the ball through his legs to level the score at 3–3.

The crowd roared their approval and Calum sprinted over to celebrate with his friend.

"Ahhh... that's better," Leo said, with an ear-to-ear grin.

The home crowd's cheers turned to excited mumbles as word spread that James Cauldfield had arrived. One by one, they turned to the corner flag nearest the playground where the star striker stood sharing a joke with an older man and Jordan's dad.

"*See*, I told you James Cauldfield was friends with my dad," Jordan shouted to anyone who would listen to him. "Now make sure you play well so I look good for the scout," he added, checking his hair – as if your hairstyle was what mattered to football scouts.

Calum wasn't really listening. He had turned his attention to Leo and Fraser. Leo was talking to the P5, pointing this way and that across the pitch. Fraser was nodding, his face a picture of concentration.

What are they *talking about?* Calum wondered.

Calum and Lewis sprinted at the opposition from the restart. Their pressure forced St Joseph's to misplace a pass, which Leo gratefully intercepted.

"Now!" Leo shouted to Fraser as he drifted towards the sideline before turning to sprint for the centre of the pitch. Fraser did exactly the same on the other side as if he was Leo's mirror image, minus the ball.

When they crossed each other's paths in the

middle, Leo laid a cheeky back-heel right into Fraser's path. Their two markers in St Joseph's sky-blue-and-white strip banged into each other like dodgems at a theme park and fell to the ground.

To the sound of people in the crowd laughing, Fraser and Leo repeated the move right in front of the goalkeeper. This time, it was Fraser who back-heeled the ball into Leo's path.

Confused, St Joseph's goalkeeper dived at Fraser's feet, losing his baseball cap in the process. But Caleytown's young winger didn't have the ball; Leo did – and he rolled it into the net to give Caleytown a 4–3 lead.

A huge roar went up from the home crowd.

"That's my boy!" Leo's dad's voice boomed out.

"Great goal Leo!" Sally and Erika shouted – they had become friends after Sally told Erika about Leo and Calum's dancing in the car.

The wind had blown Mr McKlop's hair over his glasses but he had a big grin on his face.

Calum tugged at Leo's sleeve and pointed at the older man standing with James Cauldfield. He was writing something in his notepad.

Leo grinned. "Let's make sure he puts your name in there too."

The Wonder-strike

St Joseph's were now desperate for the equaliser. Lewis and Kieran Budge were battling for the ball once again. The referee put his whistle in his mouth but had no idea who to award the free kick.

"If there wasn't a ball, this would just be a fight," Leo said to Calum, as they waited to see which cousin would win.

Eventually, the ball popped free from the stramash. Lewis and Kieran took a while to notice, but Jordan didn't stand around for either of them. He strode forward to claim it.

To catch the scout's eye, Jordan went for a spectacular long pass out to Leo's wing, and got lucky. If it hadn't been so windy, his lofted pass would have sailed out and hit someone in the crowd. Instead the wind held it up, and the ball dropped kindly into Leo's path.

Leo looked for Calum, who had his back to a defender further up the pitch. Full of confidence, he volleyed a pass forward.

With no time to think, Calum cushioned the ball on his chest.

The defender marking
him lunged forward
but Calum flicked the
ball over both their
heads. His marker fell
over, helpless, as Calum
spun round to face the goal.

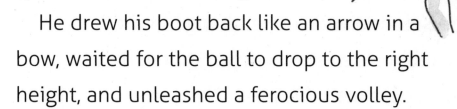

He drew his boot back like an arrow in a
bow, waited for the ball to drop to the right
height, and unleashed a ferocious volley.

The keeper didn't stand a chance.

The ball smashed the underside of the crossbar, bounced down and over the line and up again into the roof of the net. Caleytown now led 5–3; victory was assured.

A huge cheer went up from the crowd. Even St Joseph's coach was applauding. Among the cheers Calum could hear Leighton barking on the sideline and Leo laughing behind him.

"I think the scout will put that in his notebook," Leo declared.

Fraser came sprinting over. "Ace goal, Calum. Can you teach me how to do that?"

Calum laughed. "*I* don't even know how I did that!"

The referee blew the final whistle as soon as

St Joseph's kicked off. The crowd groaned: they wanted more!

Calum was gulping down water when he felt two little paws on his leg. He bent down to scratch Leighton behind his ears.

"That was some game, Calum, and some goal," his mum said.

"You must have watched your friend over there very closely on Saturday, boys." Mr Nkwanu put one arm around Leo and pointed at James Cauldfield with the other.

King's Park Athletic's striker looked up from the autographs he was signing, caught Calum's eye and waved. Jordan thought he was waving at him and waved back, then, when he realised his mistake, quickly pretended his wave was a stretch.

16

Bill the Old Scout

Sally and Erika stared, open-mouthed, at Calum and Leo chatting to *the* James Cauldfield. Jordan pretended to be busy checking out his stats on his dad's phone, but he was obviously jealous.

"Thanks for coming, James Cauldfield!" Calum said, then cringed.

"No problem... er... Calum Ferguson, we really enjoyed it, didn't we, Bill?"

The man with the notepad smiled and nodded. He was wearing a flat-cap and had a bushy white moustache. He looked old. Way older than Calum's dad and maybe even as old as Calum's granddad had been.

James Cauldfield laughed. "Sorry guys, Bill doesn't say much, but when he does speak you should listen. He knows more about football than any of us. He scouted me after all!"

Bill shook his head at James Cauldfield and looked down at his notepad. "Listen... er... Leo and Calum, is it?" Bill said.

The boys nodded like their lives depended on it.

"I'm pretty much retired now but I still do a wee bit of local scouting for King's Park Athletic."

Calum and Leo leaned in closer.

"They don't have a P6 team, but they will have a P7 squad next year."

Calum was aware that he was holding his breath.

"From what I've seen today, I'm going to tell my colleagues to come and watch you two play with an eye on next season."

Mrs Ferguson squeezed Calum's shoulder. Mr Nkwanu ruffled Leo's afro.

Calum wanted to jump up and down, shout, scream, pull his top over his head and do a lap of the pitch. Instead, he just nodded and said, "Cool."

James Cauldfield smiled at them. He knew what they were going through. "Leo, Calum, it's been a pleasure but I've got to head off. I hope to see you at the Park soon, hey?"

Calum and Leo nodded their heads again, their eyes shining like new footballs.

After the star guest had left, Caleytown Primary's players wandered back across the playground to the changing room.

With six points in the bag, their season was off to a great start, but harder tests lay ahead.

Jordan caught up with Calum and Leo. "What did James Cauldfield and the scout want with *you* two?"

Calum and Leo glanced at each other and smiled. Their lips were sealed.

Frazzler

Sending their parents on ahead, Calum and Leo decided to drop by Mr Aziz's on their way home. The changing-room door was about to swing closed behind them when Calum spotted Fraser tip-toeing down the corridor. The P5 boy froze like a deer in car headlights.

Calum glanced at Leo, who'd seen Fraser too. For a moment, nobody seemed sure what would happen next.

"Hey Frazzler, are you going to Mr Aziz's?"

Leo called down the corridor.

"Maybe," Fraser said, squinting at the name.

Calum let out a long sigh of relief.

"So are we," Leo said.

"I thought you didn't walk with P5s?" Fraser asked, inching forward now.

"Yeah, but we always walk with our teammates," Leo said. "Apart from Jordan, maybe."

Fraser almost skipped forward to meet them. "Why did you call me Frazzler?" he asked Leo.

"Because you frazzle the brains of the other teams!" Calum answered for his friend.

"Frazz-ler," Fraser sounded out his new nickname under his breath. "I like it!"

"Do you know what they call me?" Leo
asked him.

"No?" Fraser said.

Leo doesn't have a nickname, Calum thought.

"Lightning," Leo said, before pushing himself forward off Calum and Fraser's chests and sprinting in the direction of the shop.

The race was on.

DANNY SCOTT, a die-hard football fan, works for Scottish Book Trust and is the goalie for Scotland Writers F.C.

ALICE A. MORENTORN is a children's book illustrator and a teacher at Emile Cohl School of Arts in Lyon, France.

NATIONAL SOCCER SEVENS TOURNAMENT
CENTRAL WILDCATS LEAGUE

LATEST NEWS FROM MATCH DAY TWO

⚽ Muckleton take top spot in the table with a solid victory away against a very loud Hornbank Primary.

⚽ A goal feast at Caleytown! Coach Iain McKlop threw caution to the wind in the second half to ensure a glut of goals. In front of a big crowd, Calum Ferguson's spin and volley was the pick of the bunch and got him and his teammate Leo Nkwanu some attention from none other than James Cauldfield and a retired King's Park Athletic scout.

⚽ Battlehill continue to put up the barricades in front of goal with another clean sheet at home to Fieldling Primary from Tracktarry. They travel to Caleytown next for a mouth-watering match up.

⚽ Brawsome versus St Catherine's certainly wasn't a bore draw. The city slickers from Maistmore will be kicking themselves that they couldn't hold on to a 3–2 lead at home to move up the Central Wildcats table.

MATCH DAY TWO RESULTS

HOME			AWAY
Caleytown Primary	5	3	St Joseph's Primary
Hornbank Primary	1	3	Muckleton Primary
Battlehill Primary	2	0	Fieldling Primary
Brawsome Primary	3	3	St Catherine's Primary

LEAGUE TABLE

TEAM	MATCHES WON	MATCHES DRAWN	MATCHES LOST	GOALS SCORED (F)	GOALS AGAINST (A)	POINTS
Muckleton Primary	2	0	0	7	2	6
Caleytown Primary	2	0	0	7	4	6
Battlehill Primary	2	0	0	3	0	6
St Joseph's Primary	1	0	1	7	7	3
St Catherine's Primary	0	1	1	3	4	1
Brawsome Primary	0	1	1	4	7	1
Hornbank Primary	0	0	2	2	5	0
Fieldling Primary	0	0	2	2	6	0

RUMOURS & GOSSIP

⚽ Muckleton tipped as team to win Central Wildcats League.

⚽ Scout spotted showing interest in Caleytown's Leo Nkwanu and Calum Ferguson?

COMING UP: MATCH DAY THREE

HOME		AWAY
Caleytown Primary	vs	Battlehill Primary
St Joseph's Primary	vs	Muckleton Primary
Fieldling Primary	vs	Brawsome Primary
St Catherine's Primary	vs	Hornbank Primary

DESIGN YOUR OWN BADGE!

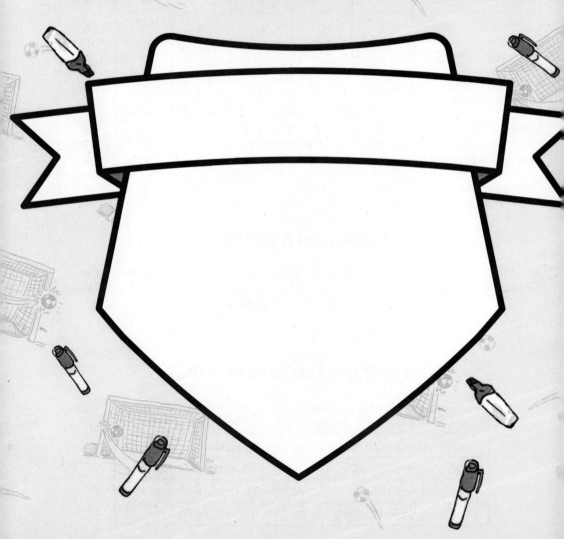

 Smash it!

Go to the edge of the box, or a reasonable distance away from goal if you're not on a pitch. With your back to goal, do keepy-uppies until you get the ball to where you want it, then turn and try a spinning volley.

 Game on!

Make this trick into a game by playing best-of-five or pretending you're each representing teams in a cup. Take turns to shoot and see who goes through to the final.

GRAB THE WHISTLE

1. A goalkeeper catches the ball directly from a throw-in. What do you do?

a) Award an indirect free kick where the keeper handled it
b) Give the opponents the ball
c) Make the goalkeeper do press-ups

If you were the referee, would you make the right call?

2. A player scores a goal straight from a corner. Do you award it?

a) Yes. Corners have the same rules as free kicks
b) Only if it looks good
c) Only if it touches the ground first

3. Instead of shooting at the goal, a player back-heels their penalty to a teammate, who shoots and scores. What do you do?

a) Run away
b) Award the goal
c) Give an indirect free-kick to their opponents

Answers: 1a, 2a, 3c